Sir Arthur Conan Doyle's

The Adventure of Abbey Grange

Adapted by: Vincent Goodwin

Illustrated by: Ben Dunn

magic wagon

visit us at
www.abdopublishing.com

Published by Magic Wagon, a division of the ABDO Group, 8000 West 78th Street, Edina, Minnesota, 55439. Copyright © 2010 by Abdo Consulting Group, Inc. International copyrights reserved in all countries. All rights reserved. No part of this book may be reproduced in any form without written permission from the publisher.

Graphic Planet™ is a trademark and logo of Magic Wagon.

Printed in the United States of America, North Mankato, Minnesota.
102009
012010

 PRINTED ON RECYCLED PAPER

Original novel by Sir Arthur Conan Doyle
Adapted by Vincent Goodwin
Illustrated by Ben Dunn
Colored by Robby Bevard
Edited by Stephanie Hedlund and Rochelle Baltzer
Interior layout and design by Antarctic Press
Cover art by Ben Dunn
Cover design by Abbey Fitzgerald

Library of Congress Cataloging-in-Publication Data

Goodwin, Vincent.
    Sir Arthur Conan Doyle's The adventure of [the] Abbey Grange / adapted by Vincent Goodwin ; illustrated by Ben Dunn.
    p. cm. -- (The graphic novel adventures of Sherlock Holmes)
    Summary: Retells in graphic novel format a story featuring the great English detective Sherlock Holmes.
    Includes bibliographical references.
    ISBN 978-1-60270-722-1 (alk. paper)
    1. Graphic novels. [1. Graphic novels. 2. Doyle, Arthur Conan, Sir, 1859-1930. Abbey Grange—Adaptations. 3. Mystery and detective stories.] I. Dunn, Ben, ill. II. Doyle, Arthur Conan, Sir, 1859-1930. Abbey Grange. III. Title. IV. Title: Adventure of the Abbey Grange.

PZ7.7.G66Si 2010
741.5'973--dc22

                                                                       2009032546

Table of Contents

Cast

Sherlock Holmes

Dr. John Watson

Sir Eustace Brackenstall

Lady Mary Brackenstall

Jack Crocker

Father Randall

The Randall Boys

Police Inspector Hopkins

Theresa Wright

4

The Adventure of Abbey Grange

December 1896 in London, England…

I'M VERY GLAD YOU HAVE COME, MR. HOLMES. AND YOU, TOO, DR. WATSON.

HELLO, INSPECTOR HOPKINS.

THIS WAS SIR EUSTACE BRACKENSTALL, I PRESUME.

EXACTLY. HE WAS ONE OF THE RICHEST MEN IN KENT.

HE'S DEAD THEN?

YES, HIS HEAD WAS KNOCKED IN WITH HIS OWN POKER.

5

HIS WIFE, LADY BRACKENSTALL, SAW IT AND HAS GIVEN US A CLEAR ACCOUNT.

YOU REMEMBER THAT LEWISHAM GANG OF BURGLARS?

I SHOULD NOT HAVE TROUBLED YOU. THERE IS NOT MUCH LEFT FOR US TO DO.

WHAT, THE THREE RANDALLS?

EXACTLY. IT'S THE WORK OF THE FATHER AND THE TWO SONS. VERY SIMILAR TO THE BURGLARY THEY DID TWO WEEKS AGO.

YES, YES, IT WAS IN ALL THE PAPERS.

I THINK WE HAD BEST HEAR LADY BRACKENSTALL'S ACCOUNT OF THE FACTS.

6

Lady Brackenstall began her tale...

"AT HALF PAST TEN LAST NIGHT..."

"...I WAS QUIETLY READING WHEN THE BREEZE OF AN OPEN WINDOW DISTURBED ME."

"I WENT TO CLOSE THE WINDOW."

"ALL SEEMED QUIET..."

7

"...THEN SUDDENLY, A FACE APPEARED."

AHHHH!

HELP! HELP!

8

HELP!

TIE HER UP!

WE NEED SOME KIND OF ROPE.

THIS WILL WORK!

"ONE OF THE MEN PULLED DOWN THE BELL ROPE AND USED IT TO TIE ME UP."

9

MMMPH! MMMPH!

WE HAVE WORK TO DO.

ARE YOU ALL RIGHT, DEAR?

10

MMMPH MMMPH!

"SIR EUSTACE RUSHED TO FIND OUT WHAT THE NOISE WAS, NOT KNOWING OTHERS WERE IN THE ROOM."

"UNTIL..."

11

"...THE MEN ATTACKED. MY HUSBAND FOUGHT BRAVELY."

WAK!

MMMPHHH!!!! MMMMMPPHHH!

12

"WITH ONE SWING, SIR EUSTACE WAS KILLED."

"FATHER RANDALL WAS TRIUMPHANT. HE STRUCK OUT AT ME NEXT."

13

"IT WAS A QUARTER OF AN HOUR BEFORE I GOT MY MOUTH FREE. WHEN I DID, I SCREAMED FOR THERESA."

OH, MA'AM!

THAT IS ALL AS IT HAPPENED.

14

ANY OTHER QUESTIONS, MR. HOLMES?

I SHOULD LIKE TO HEAR YOUR EXPERIENCE.

I WILL NOT IMPOSE ANY FURTHER ON LADY BRACKENSTALL'S PATIENCE AND TIME.

THEY MUST BE POWERFUL MEN, THESE RANDALLS.

YES, THE FELLOWS ARE ROUGH CUSTOMERS.

WHAT BEATS ME IS HOW THEY COULD HAVE DONE SO MAD A THING, KNOWING THE LADY COULD DESCRIBE THEM.

15

AND IT DOESN'T LOOK LIKE IT WAS A ROBBERY.

LADY BRACKENSTALL THINKS THEY WERE SO DISTURBED BY SIR EUSTACE'S DEATH THAT THEY DIDN'T RANSACK THE HOUSE.

NO DOUBT THAT IS TRUE.

AND YET THEY DRANK SOME WATER, I UNDERSTAND.

ONE DID TO STEADY HIS NERVES.

HA!

BUT I DON'T SEE HOW THEY CAN ESCAPE.

WE HAVE THE NEWS AT EVERY SEAPORT ALREADY, AND A REWARD IS BEING OFFERED.

16

WHAT ABOUT THIS POOR FELLOW, HOPKINS?

FROM WHAT I HEAR, HE WAS QUITE A FIEND.

THERE WAS A SCANDAL, BUT BECAUSE OF HIS STATION, THAT WAS HUSHED UP.

THEN HE THREW A BOTTLE AT THE MAID, THERESA WRIGHT. ON THE WHOLE, IT WILL BE A BRIGHTER HOUSE WITHOUT HIM.

WE'RE LEAVING?

COME, WATSON, I BELIEVE WE'LL GET MORE SOLVED AT HOME.

YOU APPEAR TO HAVE YOUR CASE VERY CLEAR.

DO LET ME KNOW WHEN THE RANDALLS ARE ARRESTED.

YOU'RE LEAVING?

17

HOPKINS SHOULD NOT HAVE TROUBLED ME, FOR THE LADY HAS GIVEN SO CLEAR AN ACCOUNT OF THE AFFAIR THAT THERE IS NOT MUCH FOR US TO DO.

WATSON, DO YOU SEE THAT?

IS THAT LADY BRACKENSTALL'S SILVERWARE? THE ONES THE RANDALLS TOOK?

NOW TELL ME, WATSON, WHAT SORT OF BURGLARS STEAL SILVERWARE AND THEN THROW IT INTO THE NEAREST POND?

At Holmes's office…

WHAT'S WRONG?

WATSON, I SIMPLY CAN'T LEAVE THAT CASE IN THIS CONDITION.

IT'S ALL WRONG. YET THE LADY'S STORY WAS COMPLETE, THE MAID'S STORY MATCHED, THE DETAIL WAS FAIRLY EXACT…

WHAT HAVE I TO PUT UP AGAINST THAT?

Holmes and Watson returned to the Brackenstall home...

WE MUST DISMISS THE IDEA THAT ANYTHING THE MAID OR HER MISTRESS HAVE SAID IS NECESSARILY TRUE.

SURELY THERE ARE DETAILS IN HER STORY THAT WOULD EXCITE OUR SUSPICION.

ANYONE WHO WISHED TO INVENT A STORY WITH ROBBERS COULD USE THE DESCRIPTIONS OF THE RANDALLS FROM LAST WEEK'S PAPERS.

IT IS ALSO UNUSUAL FOR BURGLARS TO OPERATE AT SO EARLY AN HOUR AS TEN O'CLOCK.

AND FEW BURGLARS STRIKE A LADY TO PREVENT HER FROM SCREAMING...

...SINCE THAT WOULD BE THE SURE WAY TO MAKE HER SCREAM.

AND FINALLY, IT IS UNUSUAL FOR BURGLARS TO PUT STOLEN GOODS IN A POND.

20

THE MOST UNUSUAL THING OF ALL, IT SEEMS TO ME, IS THAT THE LADY SHOULD BE TIED TO THE CHAIR.

WELL, I AM NOT SO CLEAR ABOUT THAT, WATSON. THEY MUST EITHER KILL HER OR ELSE SECURE HER SO SHE COULD NOT GIVE IMMEDIATE NOTICE OF THEIR ESCAPE.

I HAVE SHOWN, HAVE I NOT, THAT SOMETHING IS NOT RIGHT WITH THE LADY'S STORY?

21

BUT HOW DID THE BURGLAR KNOW THAT? HOW COULD HE BE SO RECKLESS?

EXACTLY, MY DEAR WATSON.

THEREFORE, HE MUST HAVE BEEN WORKING WITH ONE OF THE SERVANTS.

WHEN THIS WAS PULLED DOWN, THE BELL MUST HAVE RUNG LOUDLY.

NO ONE COULD HEAR IT. THE SERVANTS ALL SLEEP AT THE BACK OF THE HOUSE.

YOU ASK THE VERY QUESTION THAT I HAVE ASKED MYSELF AGAIN AND AGAIN.

THE FELLOW MUST HAVE PERFECTLY UNDERSTOOD THAT NO ONE COULD POSSIBLY HEAR A BELL RING IN THE KITCHEN.

22

WELL, WELL, THE POINT IS A MINOR ONE. THE LADY'S STORY CERTAINLY SEEMS TO BE SUPPORTED BY EVERY DETAIL BEFORE US.

AND YET...

WHAT?

IN THAT BELL ROPE, HE HAS GIVEN US A CLUE.

WHERE?

IF YOU WERE TO PULL DOWN A BELL ROPE, WATSON, WHERE WOULD YOU EXPECT IT TO BREAK?

AT THE SPOT WHERE IT IS ATTACHED TO THE WIRE, OF COURSE.

THEN WHY SHOULD IT BREAK THREE INCHES FROM THE TOP, AS THIS ONE HAS DONE?

23

BECAUSE IT IS FRAYED THERE?

EXACTLY!

THE MAN NEEDED THE ROPE BUT WOULD NOT TEAR IT DOWN FOR FEAR OF RINGING THE BELL. SO, HE STOOD ON THE WINDOWSILL AND CUT THE CORD.

I COULDN'T REACH THE PLACE BY AT LEAST THREE INCHES. SO, I KNOW THAT HE IS AT LEAST THREE INCHES TALLER THAN I.

THIS END, WHICH WE CAN EXAMINE, IS FRAYED. BUT THE OTHER END IS NOT FRAYED. IF YOU WERE ON THE MANTELPIECE, YOU WOULD SEE THAT IT IS CUT CLEAN OFF.

24

I SHOULD LIKE NOW TO HAVE A FEW WORDS WITH THE MAID, THERESA.

INSPECTOR HOPKINS, WHY SO GLUM?

THE RANDALL GANG WAS ARRESTED IN NEW YORK THIS MORNING.

THAT IS CERTAINLY RATHER AGAINST YOUR THEORY THAT THEY COMMITTED A MURDER HERE LAST NIGHT.

STILL, THERE ARE OTHER GANGS OF THREE BESIDES THE RANDALLS. OR IT MAY BE SOME NEW GANG OF WHICH THE POLICE HAVE NEVER HEARD.

OR PERHAPS NOT A GANG AT ALL?

25

WHAT DR. WATSON MEANS TO SUGGEST IS THAT BURGLARY MAY NOT HAVE BEEN THE MOTIVE BEHIND THE MURDER.

WHY NOT? THEY STOLE HER SILVER.

ACTUALLY, WE FOUND THE SILVER IN A POND OUTSIDE THE HOUSE.

IF THE SILVER WERE TAKEN BY PERSONS WHO DIDN'T WANT IT, THEN THEY'D GET RID OF IT.

BUT WHY SHOULD SUCH AN IDEA CROSS YOUR MIND?

WELL, THERE WAS A POND RIGHT IN FRONT OF THEM. IS THERE A BETTER HIDING PLACE?

AH, A HIDING PLACE! IT WAS EARLY AND THEY WERE AFRAID OF BEING SEEN.

SO THEY SANK THE SILVERWARE, INTENDING TO RETURN FOR IT. EXCELLENT, MR. HOLMES.

WELL, I MUST BE OFF. GOOD DAY, GENTLEMEN.

26

I HOPE... THAT YOU HAVE NOT COME TO QUESTION US AGAIN?

NO. I WILL NOT CAUSE YOU OR LADY BRACKENSTALL ANY UNNECESSARY TROUBLE. I AM CONVINCED THAT SHE IS A MUCH-TRIED WOMAN.

BUT NOW YOU MUST TELL ME THE TRUTH.

MR. HOLMES!

YOU MAY HAVE HEARD OF MY LITTLE REPUTATION.

I WILL STAKE IT ALL ON THE FACT THAT YOUR STORY IS MADE UP.

DO YOU MEAN TO SAY THAT MY MISTRESS HAS TOLD A LIE?

27

HAVE YOU NOTHING TO TELL ME?

WE HAVE TOLD YOU EVERYTHING.

ARE YOU SURE? I HEARD RUMORS THAT SIR EUSTACE THREW A BOTTLE AT YOU ONCE.

IT'S TRUE. HE HAD AN AWFUL TEMPER, WHICH WE DID NOT REALIZE UNTIL WE MOVED HERE FROM AUSTRALIA 18 MONTHS AGO.

MY LADY WAS TOO PROUD TO COMPLAIN.

GOD FORGIVE ME THAT I SHOULD SPEAK OF HIM SO, NOW THAT HE IS DEAD!

28

Holmes and Watson finished their talk with the maid and left for the docks.

THE MAID WAS LYING.

WELL, OF COURSE.

Adelaide-Southampton Lane

HELLO, I UNDERSTAND THAT YOUR LINE IS THE ONLY ONE THAT SAILS FROM ADELAIDE, AUSTRALIA, TO LONDON.

YES, YES, WE ARE.

DID ANY SHIPS FROM ADELAIDE ARRIVE HERE IN JUNE 1895?

OH, YES, LET ME LOOK. JUNE 1895... ONLY ONE SHIP, THE ROCK OF GIBRALTAR.

WAS A SIR EUSTACE BRACKENSTALL ABOARD THAT SHIP?

YES.

29

AND HIS FIANCÉE, MARY FRASER, AND HER MAID.

COULD I SPEAK WITH ANY OF THE CREW FROM THAT SHIP?

CERTAINLY.

OH, BUT I'M AFRAID THEY'RE OUT OF PORT RIGHT NOW. THEY'LL BE BACK IN A FEW MONTHS.

THANK YOU ANYWAY.

WELL, WATSON, I AM OUT OF IDEAS.

WHAT WERE YOU HOPING TO FIND?

SIR? THE FIRST OFFICER FROM THE ROCK OF GIBRALTAR, A MR. JACK CROCKER, IS STILL IN TOWN. WOULD YOU LIKE TO SPEAK WITH HIM?

30

WHY DO WE WANT TO TALK TO A SHIP'S CAPTAIN?

HE'S OUR MURDERER. OBVIOUSLY.

WHAT?!

YOU HAVE TOLD ME NOT TO QUESTION YOUR METHODS, AND I ASSUME YOU ARE PROBABLY CORRECT, AS YOU ALWAYS ARE...

...BUT SHOULDN'T WE GET INSPECTOR HOPKINS?

NO, FOR ONCE THAT WARRANT IS MADE OUT, NOTHING WOULD SAVE HIM.

LET US KNOW A LITTLE MORE BEFORE WE ACT.

CAPTAIN CROCKER, I AM SHERLOCK HOLMES. THIS IS MY ASSOCIATE, DR. JOHN WATSON.

I RECEIVED A TELEGRAM THAT YOU WANTED ME TO MEET YOU HERE.

I JUST WANT TO ASK A FEW QUESTIONS...

...ABOUT WHY YOU MURDERED SIR EUSTACE BRACKENSTALL YESTERDAY.

SIR...I THINK YOU MUST BE JOKING.

I'M AFRAID I'M QUITE SERIOUS.

32

I THOUGHT THE POLICE NEVER COULD HAVE SEEN THROUGH OUR DODGE.

SIT DOWN, MR. CROCKER.

AND THE POLICE HAVEN'T, NOR WILL THEY, TO THE BEST OF MY BELIEF.

ONLY AN ACROBAT OR A SAILOR COULD HAVE GOT UP TO THAT BELL ROPE.

AND ONLY A SAILOR COULD HAVE MADE THE KNOTS THAT HELD THE LADY TO THE CHAIR.

...AND SHE WOULD NOT HAVE LIED TO PROTECT THE KILLER UNLESS SHE LOVED HIM.

IT WAS EASY FOR ME TO FIND YOU ONCE I WAS ON THE RIGHT TRAIL.

ONLY ONCE HAS LADY BRACKENSTALL BEEN IN CONTACT WITH SAILORS, AND THAT WAS ON HER VOYAGE FROM AUSTRALIA.

WHAT ARE YOU GOING TO DO? ARREST ME?

33

NO.

I WANT YOU TO GIVE ME A TRUE ACCOUNT OF ALL THAT HAPPENED AT THE ABBEY GRANGE LAST NIGHT.

IF YOU LIE TO ME, I'LL CALL THE POLICE.

I REGRET NOTHING AND I FEAR NOTHING, AND I WOULD DO IT ALL AGAIN. BUT IT'S THE LADY, MARY--MARY FRASER--

MARY FRASER?

LADY BRACKENSTALL.

NEVER WILL I CALL HER BY THAT NAME!

I WOULD GIVE MY LIFE TO BRING ONE SMILE TO HER DEAR FACE. WHAT LESS COULD I DO? I'LL TELL YOU MY STORY, GENTLEMEN...

34

Captain Crocker told his story...

"I MUST GO BACK A BIT. I EXPECT YOU KNOW THAT I MET HER WHEN SHE WAS A PASSENGER AND I WAS FIRST OFFICER OF THE *ROCK OF GIBRALTAR*. SHE WAS SAILING TO ENGLAND WITH THAT BEAST."

"FROM THE FIRST DAY I MET HER, SHE WAS THE ONLY WOMAN TO ME."

35

"NEAR THE END OF THE VOYAGE, SHE BROKE MY HEART."

THIS CANNOT CONTINUE. I'M ABOUT TO BE MARRIED.

I AM GLAD THAT GOOD LUCK HAS COME YOUR WAY.

YOU CAN NOT THROW YOURSELF AWAY ON A PENNILESS SAILOR.

36

"MONTHS PASSED BEFORE I HEARD FROM HER OR HER MAID."

THANK YOU FOR MEETING ME. I HAD NO ONE ELSE TO TURN TO.

WHAT'S WRONG?

HE HIT HER.

WELL, I NEVER THOUGHT TO SEE HER AGAIN.

I WAS TO START ON MY VOYAGE WITHIN A WEEK.

BUT THERESA WAS ALWAYS MY FRIEND, FOR SHE LOVED MARY AND HATED THIS VILLAIN ALMOST AS MUCH AS I DID.

"I PROMISE YOU, I JUST MEANT TO TALK TO HIM. BUT WHEN I GOT THERE, THEY WERE HAVING AN AWFUL FIGHT."

DO YOU THINK I WAS SORRY? NOT I!

HOW COULD I LEAVE HER IN THE POWER OF THIS MADMAN? THAT WAS HOW I KILLED HIM.

MY LADY, DRINK THIS. IT WILL CALM YOU.

WE MUST MAKE IT APPEAR THAT BURGLARS HAD DONE THE THING.

I READ ABOUT A FAMILY OF BURGLARS IN THE AREA. CAPTAIN, WE'RE GOING TO HAVE TO TIE HER UP TO COMPLETE THE STORY.

MARY, IS THAT OKAY?

I'M CUTTING TO LOOK LIKE IT FRAYED AND THE BURGLAR PULLED IT DOWN.

39

MY LADY, REPEAT AFTER ME. THERE WERE THREE BURGLARS--A FATHER AND TWO SONS.

THE FATHER, HE HIT ME. THAT EXPLAINS THE BLACK EYE.

I'M TAKING THE SILVER TO MAKE IT LOOK LIKE A ROBBERY.

I CAN'T!

WHEN MY HUSBAND TRIED TO DEFEND ME, THEY KILLED HIM.

IS SHE GOING TO BE ALL RIGHT?

WE'LL BE FINE.

CALL THE POLICE IN 15 MINUTES.

"THEN I LEFT THE HOUSE."

"AND THAT'S THE WHOLE TRUTH, MR. HOLMES, IF IT COSTS ME MY NECK."

41

LOOK HERE, CAPTAIN CROCKER.

I HAVE SO MUCH SYMPATHY FOR YOU THAT IF YOU CHOOSE TO DISAPPEAR IN THE NEXT 24 HOURS...

...I WILL PROMISE NO ONE WILL STOP YOU.

WHAT SORT OF PROPOSAL IS THAT?

DO YOU THINK I WOULD LEAVE MARY ALONE TO FACE THE MUSIC?

GO. NO ONE WILL KNOW WHAT HAPPENED BUT WATSON AND I.

I DON'T UNDERSTAND. YOU'RE JUST LETTING THE KILLER GO FREE?

THAT'S EXACTLY WHAT I AM DOING.

IF INSPECTOR HOPKINS HAS NOT SOLVED THE CASE BY NOW, HE WON'T.

The End

42

How to Draw
Sherlock Holmes

by Ben Dunn

Step 1: Use a pencil to draw a simple framework. You can start with a stick figure! Then add circles, ovals, and cylinders to get the basic form. Getting the simple shapes in place is the beginning to solving any great case.

Step 2: Time to add to Sherlock's look. Use the shapes you started with to fill in his clothes. Use guidelines to add circles for the eyes. And don't forget the hair.

Step 3: Now you can go in with a pen and start inking Sherlock. Fill in all the details and fix any mistakes. Let the ink dry to avoid smudges, then erase any pencil marks. Sherlock is ready for some color, so grab your markers and get started!

Glossary

bell rope - a rope attached to a bell to call servants.

dodge - a trick or deception to fool someone.

fiancée - a woman engaged to be married.

fiend - a person who is very wicked.

impose - to force one's presence on another person.

Lewisham - a neighborhood in London, England.

poker - a metal rod used to stir a fire.

presume - to believe to be true without having proof.

ransack - to search through in order to commit a robbery.

reasoned - made a conclusion based on orderly, rational thoughts.

reputation - a place in public opinion.

scandal - an action that shocks people and disgraces those connected with it.

triumphant - celebrating a victory.

warrant - an official certificate that allows the police to perform an act such as a search or an arrest.

Web Sites

To learn more about Sir Arthur Conan Doyle, visit ABDO Group online at **www.abdopublishing.com**. Web sites about Doyle are featured on our Book Links page. These links are routinely monitored and updated to provide the most current information available.

About the Author

Arthur Conan Doyle was born on May 22, 1859, in Edinburgh, Scotland. He was the second of Charles Altamont and Mary Foley Doyle's ten children. In 1868, Conan Doyle began his schooling in England. Eight years later, he returned to Scotland.

Upon his return, Doyle entered the University of Edinburgh's medical school, where he became a doctor in 1885. That year, he married Louisa Hawkins. Together they had two children.

While a medical student, Doyle was impressed when his professor observed the tiniest details of a patient's condition. Doyle later wrote stories where his most famous character, Sherlock Holmes, used this same technique to solve mysteries. Holmes first appeared in *A Study in Scarlet* in 1887 and was immediately popular.

Between 1887 and 1927, Doyle wrote 66 stories and 3 novels about Holmes. He also wrote other fiction and nonfiction novels throughout his life. In 1902, Doyle was knighted for his work in a field hospital in the South African War. Four years later, Louisa died. Doyle married Jean Leckie in 1907, and they had three children together.

Sir Arthur Conan Doyle died on July 7, 1930, in Sussex, England. Today, Doyle's famous character, Sherlock Holmes, is honored with societies around the world that pay tribute to the detective.

Additional Works

A Study in Scarlet (1887)

The Mystery of Cloomber (1889)

The Firm of Girdlestone (1890)

The White Company (1891)

The Adventures of Sherlock Holmes (1891-92)

The Memoirs of Sherlock Holmes (1892-93)

Round the Red Lamp (1894)

The Stark Munro Letters (1895)

The Great Boer War (1900)

The Hound of the Baskervilles (1901-02)

The Return of Sherlock Holmes (1903-04)

Through the Magic Door (1907)

The Crime of the Congo (1909)

The Coming of the Fairies (1922)

Memories and Adventures (1924)

The Case-Book of Sherlock Holmes (1921-1927)

About the Adapters

Author

Vincent Goodwin earned his B.A. in Drama and Communications from Trinity University in San Antonio. He is the writer of three plays as well as the cowriter of the comic book *Pirates vs. Ninjas II*. Goodwin is also an accomplished journalist, having won several awards for his work as a columnist and reporter.

Illustrator

Ben Dunn founded Antarctic Press, one of the largest comic companies in the United States. His works appear in Marvel and Image comics. He is best known for his series *Ninja High School* and *Warrior Nun Areala*.